Fool Me
Once

LIZZIE MORTON

For Marla – My own little ball of chaos that adds a sparkle to each day. You came into the world and gave me the confidence to write again.

One

The cab whizzes over the Brooklyn Bridge away from Manhattan. I don't look back, but I can feel the skyscrapers twinkling deceptively as they tower upwards in the early evening sky.

The beauty of New York draws people in, fills them with hope and empty promises. It's known as the city where dreams are made, but really, it's full of lies. All it does is spit you out a shadow of your former self.

If I cared for the place even a little, I might be tempted to have one last glimpse, but I've barely been here forty-eight hours and can't wait to get away. Looking back is the last thing I want to do, so instead, I stare ahead vacantly, trying to forget everything I'm leaving behind.

Out of the corner of my eye, I catch the cab driver staring intently at me in his rearview mirror.

He clears his throat awkwardly and asks, "Anyone ever mention that you look a lot like that NFL player. Becket, I think it is. Michael Becket."

I'm used to being recognized and under normal circumstances I would humor him, maybe even sign something for him to take home and show his family, but not today. Not after everything that's happened, I'm not in the mood.

"I don't know who you're talking about," I say, dismissing him.

He shrugs and focuses his attention back to driving, as it should be.

As the traffic slows, a cab to the side catches my attention. I shift my weight, and look out of the corner of my eye, careful not to turn my head and capture the retreating city in my vision. I watch as two girls hang out of the back-passenger windows with their cells raised in the air taking selfies. Their experience of the city was clearly better than my own if they're wanting to keep the memories.

The cab driver chuckles, watching the same spectacle, and says, "I love you tourists. You remind me every day why I love the city so much. Will you be coming back soon?"

He looks into his rearview mirror, trying to catch my eye, but the last thing I want to do is engage in conversation.

"No," I reply bluntly.

Not perturbed he carries on. "Why's that?"

His chipper tone would piss me off in normal circumstances, but does so even more with the mood I'm in.

Deciding it's time to end the friendly conversation he's determined to carry on, I answer him honestly. "Because I fucking hate the place."

His glance lowers down from the mirror awkwardly and the cab returns to being silent, just the way I want it.

And that, is that.

Goodbye New York. Goodbye Abby and good riddance.

Sat in the departure lounge, waiting for my flight, I can't control my legs as they jostle restlessly. This is what being in New York does to me: it puts me on edge. I should have known better than to come, but I could feel her slipping away from me.

It didn't matter how many times I called or how many times I tried to tell her I loved her. I wasn't enough for Abby West.

The guys on the team told me months ago to sack it off when it was clear things were beginning to turn sour in our relationship. They couldn't understand why a football player living the NFL dream was so eager to be tied down. When I told them that she was the one and that I loved her, their response was, *'pussy'*.

What else would you expect from a bunch of jocks?

Hindsight is a wonderful thing and I now know I should have listened to what they were saying, rather than dismissing their opinions of the situation so quickly. Especially those of Brad, my best friend. He never quite warmed up to her and I couldn't figure out why. Maybe over the years I was so blinded by my feelings, I couldn't see what was happening right in front of me, but maybe he could.

There's something to be said for *bros over hoes*.

Muttering to myself, I pull out my cell. I could pretend I'm checking the time, which seems to have slowed down to an unbearable rate, but really, I'm looking to see if I have any messages from her.

Nothing.

The sooner I'm on the plane ordering the strongest drink on the menu, the better. Anything to quieten the memories of yesterday which are playing a constant loop in my mind.

I've spent the past twenty-four hours wallowing in self-pity, hoping she'll change her mind and decide she's made a mistake, but I would be so lucky. I could see it in her eyes, there's no going back from this for us. I knew it at the time, as we hashed everything out. Still, I found myself asking her to consider it a break and I don't know why.

As I sit, mulling over the afternoon we had at Coney Island, I realize it's possibly the worst 4th of July I've ever had. I spent the whole time watching her make love eyes at Jake fucking Ross, the guy who's been a thorn in my side for as long as I can remember. When I first hooked up with Abby four years ago, she mentioned his name, said she was heartbroken and wasn't looking for a relationship. He's always been there at the back of my mind and I've always wondered about the one that got away. That's what they call it, isn't it?

I should have known then to steer clear as she gave me all the warning signs. Even though she seemed adamant at the time she didn't want anything more, things changed. What can I say, I'm a stellar guy? Before either of us knew what was happening it was Facebook official, and we've never looked back since … or so I thought.

As time passed by, I assumed he wasn't an issue anymore and everything seemed great. That was until about six months ago, when Abby started questioning, *'The Meaning of Life'*, or some bullshit like that. She was offered two jobs, both as far away from Jacksonville, Florida as you can get. Like across an ocean far away.

Her words rang out loud like warning bells, *'What if I'm not ready for everything you want?'* They made it clear something wasn't right. If she wanted all in, marriage, kids, the works, like I did, she wouldn't have been considering either job. If you love someone, why would you want to be an ocean away?

'Have your space, Abby. Do whatever you need to do. I'm not going anywhere.' Like an idiot, those were the words I left her with.

Why couldn't I have stuck with my guns and finished the conversation the way it started, with an ultimatum? Why did I backtrack and wind up putting the power in her hands? I play for the Jacksonville Jaguars for Christ's sake. I'm one of the most sought-after NFL players in Florida, yet that scene back on the beach made me look as intimidating as a puppy.

I wish I could bang my head hard against something, scream my frustrations out loud, but then I'd chance the flight attendants thinking it was a risk letting me on the plane. There's no way I'm getting stuck here in New York. I need out of here tonight if my sanity is to remain intact. I make the decision there and then: I need to get over Abby West. I need to move on from her, because from the way she was talking, it doesn't matter how much time she has, her decision will still be the same.

A flash of blonde catches my attention. I'm not the only one whose eyes flicker upwards, focusing on the pint-sized blonde bustling through the lounge in a hurry. I smirk to myself, noticing that she looks as if she's been through the ringer. I'm not sure what's more appealing, how attractive she is with her long blonde hair and crystal blue eyes, that draw me in despite the distance between us, or the fact she looks like she's had a shitter day than I have.

I guess it's true what they say, misery really does love company.

A voice sounds out from a speaker overhead, announcing that it's time to board the flight. It breaks my concentration away from the little blonde distraction, which is for the best. The last thing she needs is the wrath of Michael Becket when he has a broken heart. My days of singledom seem like a lifetime ago, but I still remember the string of broken hearts I left behind before the beast was tamed.

It wasn't pretty.

The sooner I'm on that plane, the wheels leaving the tarmac and my broken heart behind, the better. It's not long until the city will be below me, the trip a distant memory and a hard lesson learned.

I stand, pick up my bag and make my way over to the flight attendant, flashing my e-ticket at her from my cell. I might have had to wait twenty-four hours, but I managed to get one of the last tickets. Trying to get a flight out of New York around 4th of July is an almost impossible task. It came at a hefty price, but the last thing I needed was to be stuck here any longer than necessary.

Thank God for being rich.

When I find my designated seat, I fold myself into the small space, wishing once more I hadn't taken the trip at all and put myself through the whole inconvenience. As if it wasn't painful enough having to walk away from Abby, now I have to endure over a two-hour flight in a seat with barely enough room to hold a toddler.

As I sit muttering to myself, my attention is captured by a female voice sounding out.

"Excuse me. Sorry Sir. Excuse me," I hear, as she moves down the aisle, getting closer to where I'm sat.

I glance up to see a bobbing head of blonde hair which can only belong to one person: the hot ass blonde from the departure lounge. She stops next to my seat, clearing her throat to get my attention and it seems my luck is finally improving.

In a sweet voice she says, "Sorry. I need to get to my seat."

"No problem," I drawl, then curse myself for sounding like an asshole, but I don't have the energy or the desire to make myself sound any better.

Standing, I shuffle past her in the tight space. As I do, my senses are overwhelmed by her spicy perfume, a sharp contrast to the sweet woman who keeps catching my attention.

As she slides past, her body brushes against mine and I try to ignore the excitement that courses through my veins, straight to my dick.

What can I say? I'm a guy after all. A guy that hasn't been laid in I don't know how long.

It's all I can do to stop myself humping her leg after the hot and cold performance Abby put on yesterday. I'm like a dog in goddamn heat.

She goes about settling herself in her seat and I stand for a few seconds longer. Watching the greasy guy ahead lifting his bag into the overhead luggage storage. I stare intently at his hairy stomach hanging out. Anything to stop the rage-on building in my pants. They're hard enough to hide at the best of times but shove a six foot plus guy into a confined space with a blonde bombshell and it's near impossible to disguise.

This trip keeps getting better.

"Do you want the window seat?"

The sweet voice that comes from below is music to my ears and ignoring my efforts, my dick twitches in response.

Damnit.

I shake my head, count to three then look down at her, exhaling through my nose. I must look like a madman if the crazed look on my face resembles at all how I'm feeling inside.

"I'm fine," I snap, unable to hide my irritation at the whole scenario. She looks startled by my snappy tone and I realize I need to give her a better answer. She was being nice and I'm coming across like an asshole. "I don't like the window seat."

"Everyone loves the window seat ..."

"Not when it involves looking at New York City."

She raises an eyebrow. "Who shat on your parade?"

Her cussing catches me off guard and doesn't help with the problem in my pants. It's not the kind of thing I would expect to come out of a pretty blonde like her.

"Nobody," I sigh, resigning myself to the fact I'm going to have to sit down next to her soon, as the flight attendants are completing their safety checks before takeoff.

I draw the image up again of the sweaty guy ahead, then slowly lower myself into my seat. As I move, I'm extra cautious not to present her in the face with my crotch region. The last thing she needs is a face full of that.

When I finally settle, I rest my head back against the seat and close my eyes. Sleep is what I need to forget the past couple of days, and it will help block out the blonde who is making an already painful trip home with my tail between my legs, worse.

Unfortunately, said blonde has other ideas.

"So ..." she says.

So that I don't have to reply, I try to settle my breathing to a deep, steady pace and feign being asleep.

"I know you're awake."

Opening one eye, I look down at her. "Are you always this perky?"

Speaking of perky ... when did she take her jacket off? Surely, she doesn't consider what she's wearing as clothes? My eyes flicker to the full tits staring me straight in the face. It's not even been forty-eight hours and already I'm like a horny teenager. A painful pang hits me in the chest, as remembering Abby brings the feelings of heartbreak back in one foul swoop.

"I'm not perky, just friendly. Are you always this grumpy after a breakup?"

The other eye flicks open.

How does she know I've broken up with someone? We've barely said a word to each other so it's not like I would forget mentioning it.

I say as much when I reply, giving her a suspicious look. "I never told you I'd broken up with someone."

Looking caught off guard, she clears her throat awkwardly. "It's obvious." She rolls her eyes then continues, "Nobody hates New York that much, not unless someone's made you feel that way. I simply figured out the obvious."

I contemplate what she's saying, then decide it's me making a big deal out of nothing. I'm on edge after everything that happened yesterday. How else would this perfect stranger know anything about me?

"Whatever." I close my eyes again, to make it obvious I don't want to carry on talking.

The plane jostles as it begins moving away from the departure gate, heading towards the runway for takeoff. The slight sway of the plane and steady hum of the engines begin to lull me into a slumber as the exhaustion of the past twenty-four hours kicks in.

I've almost drifted off and put all my woes behind me, when blondey has other ideas.

"So, are you headed home?"

I let out a frustrated grunt and reply, "Yep."

"Me too."

"Great."

"You're not very chatty, are you?"

She might be gorgeous and stirring up all sorts of physical responses from me, but I've had about enough of her.

I shouldn't do it, but I'm not known for my patience, so I snap back, "I've had the shittiest twenty-four hours of my life. All I want is to be left the fuck alone, not have to listen to you chatting incessantly."

It would be too lucky that a whiplashing of words would quieten her down. Instead of looking shy and meek like I'd expect, she seems overjoyed, almost ecstatic. I'm way out of my comfort zone here and she's got some next level crazy going on.

"So, you did break up with someone," she probes.

"That's none of your business."

She narrows her eyes and I pray that she might be about to give up on the conversation. It proves optimistic, as instead she gives me a sickly-sweet smile, one that makes her eyes sparkle mischievously. Despite being irritated beyond belief by her, my heart rate increases as it feels like she's staring straight into my soul. I might find her annoying, but I'd be lying if I said there wasn't something, drawing me in.

Eventually the eye contact becomes unbearable and we both look away at the same time. Unsurprisingly, she's the first one to speak again.

"I'm Britney."

I try not to scoff at her name and make myself come across as more of a dick than I already have, but I can't help it.

"How fitting." The words spill out of my mouth so quick I don't know it's happened until her expression falls.

"What's that supposed to mean?" Her demeanor changes and she begins to show another side to her bubbly personality, one that isn't quite so friendly.

"Well, you know ..."

"No, I'm afraid I don't."

"It's fitting you'd be named after a crazy ass celeb. Psycho comes to mind."

"Excuse me?" Tears well up in her eyes and I feel like shit.

I tell myself not to feel bad. I've made it clear from the get-go that I don't want to talk, and she needs to leave me alone. It's her own doing ignoring the cues I've not so discreetly given her.

"You think I'm a psycho?" she asks.

I backtrack, not wanting to turn this scenario into something beyond my control, especially when we have a full flight to endure together.

"Maybe not *psycho* per se, but you're definitely some level of crazy." The words linger in the air between us.

Instead of responding, she turns and stares out the window. It appears my words have worked their magic and I might get to continue the journey in peace after all.

Cringing to myself as I replay the past few minutes in my mind, I shake my head in annoyance at my own stupidity.

Psycho.

Who says that to someone?

An asshole like me, that's who. I close my eyes and my stomach lurches as the plane lifts off the ground, leaving New York and all my problems behind me.

17

Two

Over an hour into the journey, I come to, feeling groggy and disorientated. Hearing a slight whimper to my side, I feel like a bucket of iced water has been poured over me as I remember blonde Britney who experienced my wrath not long ago.

I could attempt to go back to sleep, but realistically it's never going to happen. I could try and fake it, anything to avoid speaking with her for as long as possible, but I'm already beginning to cramp up in the position I'm in and going to need to move soon, which will give the game away.

Rather than ignoring her like I want to, I ask, "Is everything ok?"

Another sniffle reaches my ears before she turns towards me with makeup streaked down her face.

"You're joking right?" Gone is the spritely little thing from earlier, now I'm faced with something resembling Medusa who appears to have it out for me in a big way.

Guilt creeps in as it's clear little miss sassy pants isn't quite as capable of handling my bad attitude as I thought.

There's obviously a gentler side to her that has been hurt by my nasty remarks and seeing her upset like this doesn't sit right.

"I'm sorry," I say sheepishly.

That's all it takes to settle her, and the sniffles become less frequent as we sit in silence. Only one person has ever witnessed my softer side and I left her at Coney Island with some pansy, eyeliner wearing guitarist. It's with good reason that I'm known for being ruthless on the field, the cold-hearted, ass of the team.

"I've had a bad day too."

I roll my eyes, it's a force of habit. I don't want to hear about her problems, I'm an ass like that. Most of the time I'm one hundred percent self-absorbed and not ashamed to admit it.

"Right ..." I tail off.

I don't want to ignore her, but equally don't want to engage in conversation and spend the next hour listening to her life story.

With excellent timing, the air stewardess on drinks duty makes her way down the aisle towards us. I must have missed the first round but won't make the same mistake again. I make eye contact with her and she looks surprised to see me. I would be too if I were her.

Economy isn't the place NFL players frequently reside, the main reason being the lack of space which is proving to literally be a pain in my ass. Unfortunately, there were no seats available in first, where I would have been able to stretch out and not have blondey boring my ear off.

19

The stewardess makes her way over quickly, meaning I don't have to continue my conversation with Britney.

"Two Scotches," I say gruffly. Noticing my mistake, I rectify myself. "Make them doubles." A throat clears next to me. I guess I owe her. "Make that three doubles."

"You didn't have to do that," she says sarcastically.

"Bullshit. You couldn't have made it more obvious you wanted one." She looks shocked at my pulling her up, but she's the one who decided to play this game. "Do you want it or not?"

"I guess I could settle for one."

Watching as she bats her eyelashes, I think to myself, this chick is her own brand of psycho. At least she's easy on the eye, the only thing making this whole thing bearable.

The stewardess hands over the three drinks and almost shrieks with delight when I give her a larger than normal tip. I'm feeling extra generous with the anticipation of the amber nectar about to work its way into my system. If she does another round with the cart shortly, who knows what level of friendliness I might excel to.

I quickly decide that if we're going to make it through the rest of the flight less painfully, I need to acknowledge Britney properly and make some sort of effort. I start by handing her the extra drink. "Thanks," she says, then takes a giant gulp, almost downing it in one.

I raise an eyebrow. "Thirsty?"

"I told you. You're not the only one who's had a bad day. Not that you care. You're too up yourself to bother about what anyone else is thinking or feeling."

Alarm bells ring in my head, I need to put the brakes on this conversation.

We're two strangers that have been thrown together on a plane, hovering above God knows where and she wants to delve into our thoughts and feelings? Does she think we're in some sort of romance novel?

"I'm a guy, I don't do feelings," I confirm, then take a swig from my own drink.

In the corner of my eye, I catch her gaze. It unsettles something inside me, and I can't quite decide what, so I decide to hell with it, downing the rest of my drink in one. I've a feeling I'm going to need it.

"Do you always put up so many walls?" she asks seriously, catching me off guard.

This woman is unreal. I pulled the short straw when I bought this plane ticket. It would be less frustrating if I'd paid economy prices, but with it being last minute and around 4th of July, I paid almost the equivalent to first class, to sit and put up with this crap.

The universe has well and truly got it out for me.

Deciding there's no way I'll be able to make it through the rest of the journey without my own minibar, I knock back my second Scotch, then dart from my seat in search of the stewardess. It's not a hard task when there are only two directions, she could have gone in.

I find her quickly and she doesn't bat an eyelid at my request for another large round of drinks ... perks of being famous.

She follows me back down the aisle and waits while I settle into my seat before loading the fold down table with as many drinks as she can fit. When there's no room left, I tell her to stop.

"Do you have a drinking problem?" the blonde pain in my ass asks.

"For this flight – yes."

"You're gonna be wasted. I hope you know I don't deal with puke."

I dismiss her comment, choosing not to take the bait. "I can handle my booze, thanks."

"Whatever."

She goes about helping herself to a couple of the glasses on the table, but I'm past the point of caring.

Ignoring Britney's comments about getting wasted, I knock back a couple of shots and relish in the buzz that steadily begins to hit. One of the negatives of being an NFL player is the strict diet and schedule we have to follow, which doesn't include getting wasted. It's a relief when my body and mind begin to relax as the alcohol takes over, making the woman next to me slightly more bearable.

It could be my third or fourth drink kicking in when I throw her my best panty melting smile.

"I'm sorry for earlier."

"Apology accepted," she sniffs, trying to act complacent.

The softer tone she uses shows she's not immune to my charm and it appears I haven't lost the magic touch, having been out of the game for the past four years. With my new single status, I'll be getting my practice in, starting the moment I set foot off this plane.

We sit in an amicable silence for the first time since being lumped together, and I think to myself, this I can do. Hopefully, we can spend the rest of the journey nursing our sorrows and our drinks. The universe has other plans though. Plans which involve pushing my patience to its limit when we hit a rough patch of turbulence that sends my stomach catapulting.

"Holy shit! That was bad."

We both look around at the other startled passengers. Another round of turbulence strikes.

Shit.

I pride myself on not being a nervous flyer, but this is enough to have me never setting foot on a plane again. The overhead speaker crackles and the pilots voice sounds out, informing us we're going through some turbulence, in case we hadn't noticed. As he's halfway through his safety instructions, emphasizing the importance of fastening our seatbelts, the plane lurches downwards, and I'm not talking about a little bit. It feels like we might be dropping out of the sky. The overhead lighting cuts off and the oxygen masks drop down. We wouldn't be able to see a thing if it weren't for the emergency lights.

I sit in the darkness, waiting and praying, the same thought running over in my mind.

I'm not ready to die.

Three

When I began the day, never did I imagine this was where it would lead, to me praying my life wasn't about to come to an end. The plane throws us around in the most terrifying way.

It's like something out of a movie, only it's real.

Only when I'm gripping so hard that I could be cutting off the circulation, do I notice I'm clinging to Britney's hand in sheer terror. As I loosen my grip in an attempt to let go, the plane takes another terrifying plunge downwards and passengers all around us begin screaming, Britney included.

She whimpers *'don't'* at the loss of contact when I let go of her hand.

I hesitate for a second, wondering if it's a good idea to take her hand again, but as the lurching continues, I decide what does it matter if we're all going to die anyway? Taking hold, I squeeze it in what I hope is a reassuring way.

Thankfully, the plane goes through a settled period, giving me a chance to get my breathing under control. My heartrate slows enough that I'm able to make sense of what's happening. I look around and take in my surroundings. The plane looks like it's been in an accident. I guess it all but has.

Oxygen masks hang from the ceiling; the majority of the overhead storage compartments have come open and bags are scattered along the aisles; the emergency lights continually flicker on and off.

It feels like we're in an end of the world Hollywood blockbuster, the only difference being that I can't press stop or skip past the bits I don't like.

Ironically, it's now that luck is on my side.

On the fold away table, four of the Scotches I ordered remain, looking pristine and out of place. They will help to numb what could be my final minutes on Earth. I knock one back and exhale loudly, relishing the burn and feeling of still being alive.

"You've got to be kidding me?" says Britney, her voice bringing me out of my daze.

"What?"

"We're all about to die and you're still drinking? You really are an asshole."

I'm unable to believe this is what she's worrying about in this crazy end of the world scenario.

"I never pretended to be otherwise, *Britters*." The last part I tag on purposefully to piss her off.

It works, dragging her focus away from what is happening around us, a small favor she can thank me for later ... with her mouth if she's lucky. Even to myself, in my own head, I sound like a dick.

Abby really did a number on me.

The plane jerks again, then starts to tremble over and over, causing everything to rattle. The plastic tumblers in front of me vibrate around the table at a dangerous rate. I struggle to focus as I watch them moving, unsure whether it's down to the turbulence or because I'm wasted. When I ordered the extra

25

shots from the stewardess, I didn't actually intend on drinking them all, but circumstances have changed and here we are, just about surviving.

Once more, without asking, Britney picks one up and downs it. I'm too gone to care and smirk at her action. Even in the darkness her embarrassment at her impulsiveness is visible.

"Sorry," she mumbles.

"Don't be. It's a great way to cope. I just think it's ironic you've done the exact thing you pulled me up on."

The plane lurches and she flings herself sideways, pressing her heaving breasts against my arm. Mixed with the Scotch on her breath, under normal circumstances where I wasn't fearing for my life, I'd be questioning whether I was dreaming. The effect she is having on me is a sharp contrast to earlier when all she did was piss me off.

It could be the alcohol confusing my feelings, or the situation. All I know is this attraction I'm beginning to feel towards her is the last thing I need.

Picking up one of the last two glasses of Scotch, I say, "Here."

She pulls away, breaking the contact between us which I miss instantly, and stares me directly in the eye. We seem to be stuck in a trance, forgetting everything that is happening around us. As I stare back into her icy blue eyes, I feel something change between us. Trying to ignore the feelings, I place a glass in her hands, which breaks the spell she was drawn into herself.

She replies quietly, "Thanks."

As she goes to drink, I place a hand on her wrist, and she looks at me confused. I pick up my own glass, containing my last little bit of liquid courage. The plane rumbles and I hold up my glass for what could be my last toast. "To the end."

I don't miss the glaze in her eyes, as tears threaten to spill down her cheeks. Knocking back the last shot, I relish every second of the burn as it makes its way down my throat, creating a warm buzz in my stomach. I want to feel every part of it.

If these are my last moments, I don't want to waste them.

"I broke up with my girlfriend of four years," I finally admit out loud.

I'm not sure if I say it to her or anyone who will listen. Maybe I say it to myself. Finally acknowledging what happened yesterday before I'm no more. The turbulence moves up a notch and my heart races. The calm I felt a few moments ago subsides to fear.

Britney doesn't respond to my revelation. I don't know if I expected her to. But then I find her sat, eyes tightly shut and knuckles white, as she grips the armrest between us in fright. The only helpful thing I can do is continue talking as a distraction, so I rehash the details of the afternoon at Coney Island. Even in this dire situation I'm getting pissed at the thought of Abby back in New York with Jake the asshole.

Britney squeezes my hand gently, bringing me back from the path my mind was taking. A second squeeze assures me she's been listening to what I'm saying and maybe in an odd way I've been somewhat of a comfort to her.

Another lurch, bigger than the last has her squeaking, "Shit!"

It literally is a squeak, barely audible. In her terror, all the air appears to have been sucked out of her and she's unable to speak any louder.

The slight squeeze on my hand becomes a vice-like grip, signaling how scared she is. If we weren't stuck on this godforsaken plane, which feels like it's hurtling towards the ground, I'd be enjoying the warm buzz having her skin on mine brings about. I'm not sure when I moved away from her irritating the hell out of me to this. Maybe the feelings have been there all along. Maybe there's been an underlying attraction since the moment I laid eyes on her. Now we're faced with our mortality, I'm able to see past the small details such as her incessant chattering.

Even in these circumstances, I can't help my eyes wandering over her chest, thanks to the barely there top she's wearing. I scold myself quickly. I've been apart from Abby for less than forty-eight hours and already I'm checking other women out. Am I really that guy? The guy who checks out a woman when she's stuck in a moment of panic, trying to block out everything around her.

"I'm not the perfect athlete everyone thinks I am."

She opens one eye, looking sideways at me, a signal to continue.

Seeing that my words provide a distraction from this disaster for her, I say, "I once did drugs."

Her eyebrows raise in shock and I question what I'm doing. Should I be revealing my secrets to this perfect stranger? Whatever the answer, seeing how she relaxes compared to moments ago, spurs me into a spell of verbal diarrhea.

"It was an accident. An old friend from college gave me some pain killers at a party. He was a bit of a loose cannon and I should have known better than to trust him. He got the pills mixed up, being the college supplier, and I wound up high as a kite. Luckily, it was off season, so the team didn't have any random drug testing."

I don't know what else to say or how to move forward from my revelation, but I needn't worry, as she takes a deep breath and reveals a secret of her own.

"I hate my job."

I must look crazy with the situation we're in, when I let out a chuckle and reply, "Who doesn't hate their job?"

She sighs, "No, seriously, I detest it. It's the worst job I could have chosen. I have to do things I hate, but I have no choice."

Her words are cryptic and a part of me wants to pry but now isn't the time or the place. Maybe if we get out of this in one piece, I might get the chance to ask. All I do in response is nod.

Further down the plane, the air stewardesses signal to each other frantically, all professionalism gone out the window, which can't be good. The panic on their faces is a sign something isn't right. This isn't just a little bit of turbulence. They're meant to be calm and reassuring us everything will be fine, yet they look terrified for their own lives.

Fear bubbles up inside me then without realizing what I'm doing, I begin spilling more of my darkest secrets. I need to stop, and alarm bells should be ringing. I'm one of the biggest NFL players in the country, but that's the least of my worries when it feels like the plane is plunging to our impending doom.

However, letting go of my past indiscretions is proving to be cathartic.

"I was charged with assault in high school."

Britney's head whips around, knowing the secret I've chosen to divulge is huge. If the NFL caught wind of this, everything I've worked for over the years would come under question. I've told her my worst and I don't know why.

Drugs.

Assault.

These things could ruin my career, yet here I am, trusting her like it's my final confessional before God. Maybe in some way it is.

I had reservations about her earlier, but she's endearing in her own way. There's something drawing me in, and it appears I no longer have control over my actions.

Especially when she cries out, "I'm a virgin!"

All I do is blink.

Those were the last words I expected to come from someone like her. Someone so ... hot.

I don't have time to think about what she's revealed, as the plane dips and my stomach feels like it's about to bottom out. I might be sick from the anxiety surging through me, and I genuinely think to myself, *we're about to die.*

Rather than wasting my last moments worrying about the implications of my actions, I lean forward and press my lips to hers. A spark of electricity surges through me. It's as if this is the place my lips were always meant to be, on hers. Lost in the comfort of her pressed against me, nothing else matters and maybe without noticing, I've died and gone to heaven.

I open my eyes and pull away steadily, looking around and wondering whether I've passed over to the other side. Did I miss the moment when the plane plummeted to earth and crashed? If I did, then being lost in Britney was a hell of a way to go.

Britney remains sat, eyes closed, her breathing heavy. There's another drop, evidence we're still stuck in this nightmare. Screams ring out all around us and I decide I'm going to kiss her again and refuse to come up for air until we're safe.

I've decided my fate. I want my life to end feeling those full, warm lips and experiencing every sensation she makes soar through my body.

Leaning back in, I kiss her again and my senses become overloaded with her spicy perfume, which I now know is fitting with her sassy attitude. She's the type of girl you want to take to bed and do unthinkable things with all night long. In fact, scrap the bed, I'd do her anywhere any time, all she'd have to do is say the word and I'd be putty in her hands.

As we continue kissing, another smell hits me, one unique to her. Vanilla and honey, her true scent and fitting with the little secret she let slip. It's evidence that underneath her bitchy bravado is an innocent young woman. One who's scared for her life and kissing me back like these are her last moments on earth, which they very well might be.

We get into our own rhythm and time seems to disappear. Everything around us settles, like the world is at peace and all is right now we're in each other's arms. When the emergency lighting flickers off and the cabin becomes illuminated once more, I realize it's in fact because the turbulence has passed, and we might finally be safe again. Everyone around us gasps in relief but I'm still lost in all things Britney.

God, I wish we were anywhere but stuck on this plane and I could show her exactly how much I appreciate her.

Reluctantly, we pull away from each other, at the same time the speakers above crackle to life, with the voice of the Captain again. He spends a few minutes explaining that the plane passed through a storm which caused the extreme turbulence. The air stewards go about tidying up the mess from the *'turbulence'* and he finishes by apologizing for the inconvenience, as if it were simply a hiccup in the journey, not seeming to care we all thought we were about to die.

I snort to myself in amusement. Thankfully, most of the flight is done with and shortly we will begin our descent to land. Next time I need to go anywhere, no matter what it's for or how long it takes, I'm taking the road. There's no way I'm setting foot on a plane any time soon. Time with a therapist could also be on the cards.

I look at Britney, taking in her flushed appearance after our near death make out session, loving that I'm the one who did that to her, made her feel that way.

Leaning down, I whisper in her ear, "You good?"

She startles at my proximity and for a second, I wonder if I've misread the situation by speaking to her intimately. My defenses rise, the same ones she smashed apart with those soft lips of hers just minutes ago.

"Sorry," she says, her embarrassment obvious. "I was in a daydream."

"That was a bit crazy huh?" I try to keep my tone light and avoid any awkwardness.

The way she swallows nervously is evidence she's thinking back to the moment we shared together and seems as unsettled by it as I am. I'm not the only one who felt the spark. I can tell by the color of her skin, the wild look in her eyes and the way she's still panting, even though a few minutes have passed since we parted. My gaze moves down to her lips and I wonder whether now we're no longer going through a near death experience, it would be acceptable to try and kiss her again or if the moment has passed.

It feels like a lifetime ago I was racing out of New York, determined to get away from the city I hate. I'd been avoiding anything that reminded me of Abby who I thought was the love of my life, yet here I am lusting after a complete stranger like a lost puppy.

Somehow, I've gone from being the one in control in this scenario to completely out of control and I'm not sure how I feel about it. That's not including the secrets we shared and the implications there will be if she chooses not to keep them between us. All I can do is pray that this Britney isn't quite as psycho as I imagine the real one to be.

"Listen ..." comes the famous word, with a tone that would be recognizable to many.

The same tone that says, *'I like you but...'*

The last thing I need to finish off the day is to have my man card revoked, so I hold up a hand with a sheepish smile on my face, urging her to stop.

"No hard feelings," I say. "We were caught up in the moment. Let's leave it at that."

The relief that floods her features, is so clear I try not to be insulted, but can't help feeling irked. There's no way she didn't feel the same about that kiss. Chemistry like that can't be made up. Then again, I thought Abby and I were made for each other which I was wrong about. Maybe my judgements aren't to be trusted.

She gives me a warm smile, her demeanor changing entirely and throwing me off. "What are you doing when we land?"

It's the last thing I expect her to ask when she basically dismissed the kiss we shared as nothing.

"After that... I need a strong drink, or ten. So, I'll be heading straight to a bar. You?"

"Maybe I could join you?"

I look at her skeptically after she's changed her tune so suddenly.

"Don't get me wrong, I would love your company, but I'm a guy and sometimes you have to spell things out for us. I'm a little confused what's going on here."

"We almost died together. The least we could do is share a drink ... or ten," she echoes my words with a glint in her eye.

Something's changed and she seems different to the Britney I spent the plane journey with. Her mouth says one thing, her face another, she seems reluctant, as if this situation is out of her control.

The words come out of nowhere when I ask, "Do I know you from somewhere?"

It's been bugging me since I first laid eyes on her back at JFK, the sense I know her, I'm just not sure how.

Like a deer caught in the headlights, the remnants of the flush from our kiss disappear as she visibly pales then swallows nervously.

"I know you from the TV. You're the big sports guy, aren't you?"

There I was thinking she didn't have a clue who I was. Maybe this is the reason she seems reluctant to take things further after our kiss. She could be one of those crazy chicks who finds the whole fame thing a turn off. Not that I would blame her, I still find it all intimidating sometimes.

I nod and look ahead. Warning bells are finally ringing and they're probably too late. Something doesn't feel right. After the secrets we shared, secrets I've never told a soul because they could ruin my career, my guard is up. I need to be more careful.

"So, how about that drink?" she asks sweetly.

What harm could a drink do with a hot chick after what we've been through. It was on my agenda anyway.

"Sure," I reply, while observing her long blonde hair and bright blue eyes.

My brain and my dick are at an impasse and only one will come out winning.

If only I knew the implications of my decision.

Four

Britney looks at me and asks, "Do you not have people for things like that?"

I look down at her in amusement, as I stand on the sidewalk with my arm extended, attempting to catch a cab for the both of us. We're headed to the same place, so it makes sense we catch a ride together.

I dismiss her assumptions and reply, "I like to keep things as normal as possible."

She doesn't need to know about the huge bachelor pad awaiting my return. The one that finally gets to live up to its reputation now I'm pretty much a free agent.

"That's cool." She scuffs her toe against the sidewalk, showing she's nervous and doesn't know what else to say.

A cab screeches to a halt in front, saving us from the awkward silence. I busy myself by loading up the trunk with our bags, before sliding into the back-passenger seat beside her. I reel off the name of a familiar bar to the driver, something which isn't local so I can drink in peace.

And then we sit. You could cut the tension with a knife. The minutes ticking by feel like hours and I pray we don't hit traffic. We shouldn't do at this time of night. The driver hums to the radio in the front, sheltering us from listening ears.

Becoming frustrated with the whole situation, I ask, "Is everything ok? You seem a bit weird?"

Her eyes snap to mine. "Weird? Thanks."

Her gaze returns to the window, watching the buildings as we quickly pass by.

I rub a hand down my face in frustration, wondering whether this is worth the effort. Should we just part ways?

Still, I can't deny the feelings that surfaced when I kissed her on the plane, which encourages me to say, "Sorry. I don't mean weird as in *you're* weird. I mean it's weird that after our kiss on the plane, it's like we're back to being strangers."

"That's because we are strangers," she replies without returning her gaze to mine.

She has a point.

"Ok. Do you want me to get out? I can get a different cab and we can pretend like this never happened?"

She exhales, "I can't believe I told you I was a virgin."

I blink rapidly as what she says registers. Her change in mood begins to make sense.

"Is that what this is about?"

"Er ... yeah."

"Being a virgin isn't anything to be embarrassed about." I hear myself speak and wonder where this nice, understanding guy has come from. It's out of character for me to say the right thing at the right time, usually it's the other way around. "It's kind of cool," I remark.

She focuses her attention back on me. "Cool? What do you mean, cool?"

"A lot of guys like that kind of thing. It's a turn on."

Groaning, she begins dramatically banging her hands against her head.

"Telling you was a ridiculous thing to do."

Just like that Britney is back to being unreadable, and I have no idea what she's getting at.

"Let me get this straight. I've just told you guys like that sort of thing and you're still embarrassed?"

"No, not embarrassed. I'm frustrated you know because now it's a challenge."

Bewildered, I ask, "A challenge how?"

"It's like in the movies. People find out the girl's a virgin and suddenly it becomes every guy's goal to try and steal her v-card, then brag about it to the world."

Deny, deny, deny.

"You watch too many chick movies."

She has a point, not that I'm going to admit it. I'd like to say it doesn't happen, but it does. More than once I've been a witness to locker room talk. Over the years I've been with Abby, I've become the listener, as the guys bragged about their conquests and occasions where they've taken a girl's virginity. Still, it's wrong for her to assume that would be the case with me.

"You shouldn't judge people you don't know," I say.

There's some irony in what I'm saying, considering I lumped her in the same category of crazy as another kind of Britney, not that I'm about to 'fess up to it.

Her shoulders sag and I know she hears the truth in what I'm saying. "Sorry. It's a sore subject."

"Clearly." I don't expand further, wanting to move on from what is quickly becoming an awkward conversation. "It's nothing a few drinks won't solve, right?"

My buzz from the plane is beginning to wear off. That, mixed with the post-adrenaline come down of almost dying, has my head pounding.

"You still want to have a drink with me, even after I've acted all crazy?" She lets out a small laugh, attempting to lighten the mood.

"Crazy is my name and crazy is my game."

She throws her head back, this time laughing genuinely. I swallow hard at the spectacle that is Britney letting her walls down. It's beautiful to watch and has me feeling things I'd be hesitant to admit out loud.

"I can't believe you just said that."

"Neither can I." Truthfully, I'd say it a hundred times over if it meant I got to watch her let her guard down and laugh like that again.

The cab pulls to a sudden halt.

I'd become so focused on the conversation that I hadn't noticed the journey passing by. I'm not overly familiar with the area and feel slightly disorientated, but a quick glance out the window confirms we've arrived at the bar where I asked the driver to drop us off. I pull a wad of cash from my pocket and hand over a few bills, telling the driver to keep the change.

I hold my hands up, refusing her offer of splitting the bill when Britney tries to help.

"Fine," she says sternly. "First round is on me."

When the money is settled, we exit the cab at the same time and I move to the trunk, popping it open and removing our bags. I'm surprised that Britney's luggage is even smaller than my own.

"Light packer?" I ask.

Even Abby, the least fashion driven girl I know, would pack a larger bag than Britney. I find it a little odd and wonder to myself what exactly she was in New York for.

She shifts awkwardly, seeming put off by my comment. Grabbing the bag out of my hand she replies, "It was a flying visit."

"Obviously." I choose to leave it, the need for a drink stronger than my need to pry. Instead, I close the trunk, turn, and head into the bar with her following closely behind.

Once inside we find a table and set our bags underneath. The bar is virtually empty with it being the day after 4th of July. This isn't the kind of place people come to around this time of year, usually you'd find them partying at the beach or a lake somewhere. It means I can drink almost alone, undisturbed by fans and without the worry of *paps* hanging around, attempting to catch me up to no good. Not that they'd have much luck as I avoid them like the plague.

Apart from the few indiscretions I revealed to Britney on the plane, I keep my behavior in line.

I have to.

I sit down and make myself comfortable. Britney looks at me surprised.

"You said drinks were on you." I smirk, knowing I'm coming across as a dick but I'm back to not caring.

She's been standoffish since our kiss on the flight and I'm running out of steam when it comes to putting in any effort.

She nods then asks, "What would you like?"

"A couple of beers. And a few rounds of Scotch." She looks surprised by my larger than normal drink order. My plan for the night involves letting off steam after the hellish couple of days I've had. The flight was the icing on the cake and the only way I'll be capable of chilling out is by drinking – a lot.

I can't help my eyes travelling up her jean clad legs as she makes her way to the bar. They settle on her pert, round ass which I didn't get a chance to appreciate earlier. What I wouldn't give to have that ass in my hands. I try to ignore the thoughts. If she continues the way she is, there's no chance things will go further with us.

A few minutes later, she returns with a tray full of drinks and it's my turn to be surprised.

"Thought I'd join in with the party." It's the friendliest she's been since we got off the plane, showing a possibility that she may be decent company for the night.

I pick up one of my beers and take a long swig, relishing the coolness as it makes its way down my throat and the stress from earlier begins to seep away. All the while Britney never takes her eyes off me. They bore into my own and I feel the same buzz from earlier beginning to take ahold. She swallows nervously, proving once again that it's not just me affected by our connection.

I refuse to take my eyes away from hers as I pick up one of the shots and knock it back. I'm transfixed as she licks her lips, watching me, unaware of the reaction her body is having.

"So ..." I say, attempting to break the silence and begin a conversation, before I'm tempted to lean over the table and finish what we started earlier.

Virgin or not, psycho or not, if I could have my way, she'd be screaming my name before the night is out.

"That flight was crazy, right?" She looks down nervously, then picks up one of her drinks and takes a sip.

I take a swig of my beer to chase down the Scotch. "My worst fucking nightmare is what it was. It'll be a long time until I set foot on a plane again."

She looks taken aback by my honesty. It's not surprising, considering I'm a six foot plus linebacker, admitting to now having a serious fear of flying.

"It was scary. I thought for a moment we were done for."

"Don't remind me," I moan. It's too soon to relive the memories. I make quick work of another shot then ask, "Is that all you got?"

Only one drink remains on the tray which I assume is hers.

"This is all you asked for," she says bluntly.

"Right ..." I reply, then stand and stalk to the bar.

I'm beginning to feel like a hormonal teenager the way my mood is jumping all over the place. Being in a near plane crash shortly after breaking up with your girlfriend of four years will do that to you.

"Three Scotches," I say to the barman, not caring that he looks at me suspiciously.

He clearly recognizes who I am, but with the mood I'm in, I couldn't care less. The alcohol is kicking in from the previous few drinks and I'm feeling invincible, not caring about my actions. When he returns with my drinks, I throw down some money on the bar, then head back to the table where Britney is typing away on her cell frantically.

She startles and shoves it away into her pocket as I sit back down.

"I didn't mean to disturb you. Something urgent?"

"No ..." she stammers.

For a moment I wonder why she looks guilty. It might be the cynic in me, but despite the undeniable attraction I feel towards her, there's something about this chick that doesn't sit right. Under normal circumstances I'd be wary, but today has been utterly shit and I don't see how having drinks with a beautiful stranger can make it any worse.

I slam back another shot, to which she comments, "You're going to wind up wasted."

"Not your problem," I snap.

"You're back to being an asshole again?"

"And?"

"I thought a near-death experience might make you more likeable, but I was obviously wrong. I shouldn't have come here."

Crossing her arms across her chest, she lets out a huff. All it does is draw my attention back to her breasts, and in the drunken haze that's beginning to settle in, my eyes lazily trail over her body.

"Seriously?" she all but barks at me. "You really are gunning for douchebag of the year."

"Breaking up with someone will do that to you." I don't need to explain myself, but I do. After all, she made the effort to come here with me.

My words soften her demeanor somewhat and I hate that for a second, she looks like she pities me.

She confirms it when she says, "I'm sorry."

I don't need her pity.

"Don't be. There's plenty more pussy out there."

Her face visibly reddens, but it's not out of awkwardness or embarrassment, it's because she's angry.

"You have a way with words."

I knock back another shot, dribbling slightly and wiping away the excess liquid with the back of my hand as the room tilts. This isn't normal. I may have packed away my fair share of alcohol, but I'm also a big guy and it takes more than this to get me wasted. Shrugging the thought to the side, I slur, "I never pretended to be a gentleman."

43

She narrows her eyes, which once again draw me in and send my pulse racing.

"Excuse me for a moment. I have to use the restroom." She shoves her chair back and walks away from the table.

I sit for a second wondering what I'm doing. Even by my standards I'm acting like a dick, but I can't control it. Word vomit keeps pouring from my mouth. There's only one person to blame for how I'm behaving, and I left her back in New York. The room sways again but I shrug it off. I came here with the intention of getting wasted and drowning my sorrows. Who cares if it happened quicker than expected?

A sudden urge to follow Britney takes over. I want to give her a piece of my mind and tell her exactly how much her hot and cold attitude is pissing me off, so that's exactly what I do.

Standing up, I sway on my feet as I head towards the restrooms. I stand outside the female door for a second and question whether I should knock to forewarn her I'll be coming in. Acknowledging that she's seen me in all my asshole glory, I think to hell with it and opt to barge straight in.

When I enter, she's stood at the washbasin, looking at herself in the mirror. She pulls back in horror when she sees it's me who's barged my way in.

"What do you think you're doing?"

"You."

I'm not sure where the forwardness comes from or when the plan changed, but I don't care. I stalk towards the small, sassy blonde who's been playing games with me since I laid eyes on her in New York. Reaching out, I grab her waist firmly and drag her in towards me. She doesn't resist, not even for a second and I'm relieved that despite my dickish comments, I

44

haven't scared her off. All I've done is add fuel to the fire.

Nothing could prepare me for the series of explosions that fire through my body when our lips meet. If I thought our kiss on the plane was memorable, it's nothing compared to being in the privacy of the restroom, with no watchful eyes and no arm rest acting as a barrier between us.

My dick stands to attention when she lets out a moan, and I feel like I've died and gone to heaven when her tongue meets with mine and the kiss deepens. I'm not sure if it's the alcohol making me this bold, or it's a side she brings out of me, but I begin kissing her like I've never kissed anyone before. My hands wander and explore her body, hesitantly at first … after all, she did just tell me she was a virgin. I don't want to push her or make her do anything she isn't ready for, even though I'm dying to feel what it's like being inside her.

When my hands find the peachy ass, I couldn't take my eyes off a few minutes ago, I grab it firmly and lift her. She wraps her legs around my waist, and I sit her back against the countertop. Leaning in, I try to get as much contact between our bodies as possible. A ringing in my ears starts, that I struggle to block out and I can't stop myself falling against Britney as the room tilts and sways.

I try to regain my footing but it's a wasted task. My limbs have turned to jelly and the last thing I'm aware of, is my face planting firmly into her cleavage like it's a giant pillow and mine for the taking.

Five

An annoying buzz keeps repeating itself over and over. I lie listening, then groan.

Seriously, what the fuck is that noise? It's making the pounding in my head seem a thousand times worse. When it stops, it provides a temporary relief, but then it starts again.

I moan into my pillow, "Why won't it stop?"

A murmur next to me makes me freeze and my blood runs cold. The sheets draped over me rustle and I daren't move. The first thought that runs through my mind is what have I done? I can't have cheated on Abby, not after all this time. I'm not that kind of guy.

Then I remember the past couple of days, the longest of my life. There was the break-up with Abby as Coney Island, thanks to Jake, the one who got away, or whatever the fuck it was. Then there was possibly the most expensive flight I've ever booked, in an attempt to get away from New York City as fast as possible. That same expensive flight almost ended my life and has potentially put me off air travel permanently.

I remember getting wasted drinking Scotch with Britney. Beautiful, blonde Britney. Britney with the sassy mouth, who had her own level of crazy going on with her hot and cold mood swings. Britney the virgin. Although by the looks of things, the fact I'm naked in bed and the last thing I remember is face planting those beautiful breasts of hers, means she may not be a virgin any longer.

The bed moves again, and I dare to lift my head, preparing myself for the vision of long blonde hair flowing in front of me. I'm shocked when instead I find familiar brown hair, attached to a petite frame that looks an awful lot like Abby's.

My mind works at a million miles an hour and a moment passes where I think to myself, *'was it all a dream?'* Maybe I hit my head and the past few months haven't happened and Abby and I are still in our bubble getting on with our lives together. It's a hopeful moment, but I quickly notice as my eyes trail over the body next to me, that the bed we're in, isn't in fact mine.

Taking a deep breath, I dare to glance around and take in the rest of my surroundings. Judging by the run-down furniture and art décor style interior, I've found my way into some sort of motel room. Now all I need to figure out is who I'm very naked in bed with.

I clear my throat awkwardly, which proves painful. I don't know what I was up to last night, but my throat feels like I've swallowed glass. The body next to me rolls over, and I'm faced with an incredible pair of breasts. I try not to stare, willing my body not to react but it has other ideas. Opting to protect the owner's modesty, I gently pull up the covers when my attention is drawn to her face. No one could say I don't have a type. As I gaze at her features, I acknowledge that the similarity to Abby is uncanny.

Whoever she is, it appears she isn't waking up any time soon, so, deciding I've had enough of waiting round to find out what's going on, I nudge her until she begins to stir. She lets out a small moan, that again my body responds to.

Finally, her eyes flutter open, clouded in a sleepy haze.

"Morning," she sighs.

I try to keep my expression friendly, but I'm mortified that I can't remember how we got here or what happened.

Sheepishly I say, "I'm sorry, who are you?"

The potential of a cozy morning after flies out the window, as she sits up clutching the sheets around her awkwardly.

"Please tell me you're kidding, right?"

I want to say yes, pretend I was joking, but it would be wrong to lie to her. Plus, there's no hiding that I haven't got a clue what her name is or where we are.

"I'm not," I admit. "I'm sorry."

"Oh, my gawd," she groans into her hands, hiding her face from mine. "I can't believe I let this happen. I knew you were wasted but I thought we were all just having a good time. I didn't realize you were *that* bad."

"It's not your fault," I say, trying to reassure her, but I'm feeling shit about the whole scenario myself.

"I feel like I took advantage of you. Oh God, please don't tell anyone. I can't believe I took advantage of an NFL player."

I don't know what the big deal is. If any other girl were in her shoes they'd be jumping for joy, ready to run to the press and sell the story for a big buck. I pray that's not what she's going to do, or Coach will have my ass.

"You didn't do anything wrong. I mean it's obvious I was too wasted to remember anything, but it's not your fault. It's what everyone does ... right?"

"Don't you have a girlfriend though?"

It's a simple question, but one that alerts me to the fact that although I don't know who this girl is, she knows plenty about me.

"Not anymore."

She lets out a relieved breath. "At least I won't be blamed for destroying your relationship."

"Believe me, it wouldn't have taken much to destroy it, even if we hadn't broken up a couple of days ago."

"A couple of days ago?" she asks looking alarmed. "So, you're on the rebound? God, I'm such an idiot. I thought you liked me, but really you were looking for someone to get under you so you could forget about her."

"Believe me, that's not what happened here. I mean, I'm not exactly sure what happened, but if I was going to try and use anyone to get over her, it wouldn't be you."

Her nostrils flare with anger, and for a moment I think she might slap me.

"You're a douchebag you know that?" She dives off the bed taking the sheet with her, leaving me completely naked.

At first, I think she's having a typical chick freak out, then it clicks that she's upset by what I said.

"Shit! I didn't mean it like that."

Standing up quickly from the bed, I grab a pillow to try and cover my modesty, then make my way over to her, where she's frantically attempting to pull on her clothes which are scattered around the room.

"Hey ..." I say soothingly, hoping some of her anger will subside. She stills at the gentleness in my

49

voice which, given how crap and irritated I feel by the whole scenario, surprises even myself. "I didn't mean anything offensive by what I said." She swallows and the tears in her eyes make me feel like an even bigger prick. "What I meant was, you look just like her. If I wanted to get over her, it wouldn't be with you because you're too similar."

Her shoulders drop as some of the tension leaves her body.

"Ok," she says meekly, then continues putting her clothes back on, much to my disappointment. "I'm sorry for going crazy. I don't normally do this and when you showed up at the party last night, me and my friends got excited, and they egged me on. I never thought we'd actually hook up, but I was drunk too. I'm a bit embarrassed."

"Believe me, you're not the only one. You have nothing to be embarrassed about."

I smile down at her, wishing we were in a different situation and could continue our morning in bed together. But my head is pounding, and I need to get home, which will prove difficult considering I don't have a clue where I am or where any of my things are, including my bag from the flight.

I leave my lady friend to carry on dressing and move around the room gathering my own pieces of clothing. I slowly put them on, careful with my movements, not wanting to chance vomiting in female company.

"This is going to officially put me on your asshole list, but I have no idea what your name is ..." I hope she notices I'm talking to her and not the wall I'm facing.

"It's Lola."

Thankfully, she doesn't sound any more pissed off than earlier.

"I'm sorry about all of this," I mutter as I shove my hand in the pocket of my pants, finding my wallet and my cell.

Luckily, my cell still has battery left. As I unlock it, it becomes clear this was the offending object making all the noise, as my screen registers dozens of missed calls and messages.

Once again, I wonder what happened last night. I didn't land in Florida until after nine, then had drinks in the bar with Britney, although I'm beginning to think she was a figment of my imagination. I register that it's just after nine AM.

If I went for a couple of rounds with the lovely Lola, logistically that gives me a maximum of six hours unaccounted for. I can't have gotten up to too much in that time. I may have had a few drinks and blacked out, but generally I'm pretty strait laced. Even when I'm wasted, I behave. I pray that was the case last night, as it's been a long time since I've woken up unable to remember anything.

Not wanting to drag things out any longer than necessary, I finally ask Lola the question I've been dreading most of all. "So ... where exactly are we?"

I can feel my body tensing as I await her answer, then she turns and looks at me with a friendly smile.

"We're in Georgia silly. How could you forget?"

Motherfucker, what have I done?

Six

My teammate Brad looks at me bewildered.
"What were you thinking man?"
"I wasn't. I think that's pretty obvious."
I roll my eyes as we repeat the conversation we've had twice since he picked me up in Georgia.

Normally, being dragged between states he'd be beyond pissed, but this is me and it's the first time I've ever done anything like this. He found the whole thing hilarious, yet we still find ourselves creeping back to the more serious line of conversation. A lot is on the line and doing something like this, especially right before football season was a huge risk, regardless of whether I was aware what was happening or not.

So far, I've been too hungover to go into any more details about what happened, so it doesn't come as a shock when he finally broaches the subject.

"What happened yesterday and how the fuck did you end up all the way in Georgia?"

"Long or short version?"

"Whichever version means I get the full story."
Focused on driving, he continues staring intently at

the highway in front of us, but he's hanging onto my every word.

"Abby broke up with me."

"Damn." His nostrils flare. He's thinking about the implications this will have for him and the team, how it might affect my performance for the upcoming season. "Do you know why?"

"Don't pretend like we didn't all see it coming. She's been distant for months, but that asshole from back in high school definitely had a part to play."

"I'm sorry man. You're better off. Did it really warrant an all-out bender that landed you all the way in Georgia though? Do you even know how you got there?"

"No and no," I answer.

Looking out the window I wonder if I should tell him the rest of the story. He might be one of my closest friends, but I tend to keep a lot of stuff to myself and under normal circumstances I'd hold back. I have a bad feeling about all this though, something in my gut is telling me things don't add up and I'm dreading what the fallout might be.

What really happened last night will come out of the woodwork. Shit like this always does and when that happens, I'm going to need Brad and my team by my side to deal with it all and help clean up the mess.

"It didn't help being stuck in New York. You know what that place does to me."

He frowns. "Not an excuse for getting wasted like you did."

"How about being on a plane that almost crashed?"

"Wait – what?" He turns slightly, still keeping control of the car, glancing quickly to try and read my expression and see whether I'm being serious.

"I'm not joking. We went through a huge spell of turbulence. Emergency lights, the works, for over ten minutes. The damn thing kept lunging towards the ground and people were screaming. I thought I was going to die."

"Shit," he says, exhaling. My story has obviously unsettled him. "Why didn't you message me?"

"I was too focused on getting a drink. You were on my agenda, however a pretty blonde got in the way."

"Did you also lose your vision in the past couple of days? Lola was brunette, like Abby."

"I know that. It's what's confusing me in all this. The last thing I remember is making out with a girl called Britney in the restroom. She was blonde, beautiful and the complete opposite of Abby. I keep trying to remember what happened, but it won't come to me."

Brad chuckles and the sound fills the car. I thought he might have been more pissed with me, but his reaction says otherwise.

"Give it time. You're out of practice and you've forgotten what hangovers are like. The memories will come back soon."

"You think?"

"I know."

I wish he were right.

I wish the memories did come back and all of this was the result of a drunken night out, but that would be too simple. Ever since I set foot in New York my life has become complicated and anything but normal.

If only I knew exactly how messy it was about to get.

Seven

The following couple of weeks fly by and my indiscretions from 4th of July lurk in the background. Luckily, nothing comes of them, but the memories have yet to reappear which makes me nervous.

It's also a couple of weeks since I spoke to Abby and our breakup status remains unclear. I decide it's time to confront her, not face to face, there's no way I'm making my way back to New York, even if it is for Abby. In the end, I opt for calling her.

Now, sitting in the locker room as I lace up for practice, I wish I hadn't bothered. It proved a waste of time and effort. I don't know why we didn't end things properly to begin with. I was an idiot to ask her for more time, knowing the result was inevitable. I never stood a chance with so much distance between us for so long, never mind with Jake hovering around.

Frustrated, I throw my clothes into my locker, slam the door and storm out of the room with the wary glances of my team following me. I'm raging and hope that rather than letting this whole mess drag me down, I might be able to vent my frustrations into my performance at practice. I never get a chance, as Coach planned the most vicious practice we've had to date. The perk of it being so tough, that I didn't have a chance to think about anything, not even Abby.

"That was brutal," complains one of my teammates as we hobble back into the locker room a few hours later.

"I wonder what's crawled up his ass. He was on one today," agrees Brad.

"Beats me," I say. "I'd be happy if we didn't have a repeat of that for a while."

My body screams out in protest as I slowly lower myself down onto the bench, each muscle crying out in agony. Leaning back, I rest my head against the cool metal of the locker behind, struggling to find the energy to shower.

Suddenly the room fills with the sound of everyone's cells ringing and bleeping continuously. "What's going on?" I ask Brad.

He stands frowning, his cell in hand, staring intently at the screen. For a second, he looks furious and then bursts out laughing. Looking around, I feel unsettled as I watch the rest of the team do the same. Somehow, I know it's about me and what happened the day I returned from New York.

My gut is kicking up a stink and it isn't wrong.

"Well?" I ask hesitantly.

I'm not entirely sure I want the answer. Brad doesn't answer, just shakes his head as his eyes fill with tears of laughter before he hands over his cell. I take it reluctantly, then spend a moment or two working up the courage to finally look down and see what has captured everyone's attention.

Nothing could have prepared me for what I see. A mixture of nausea and rage hit in multiple waves as the guys on the team line up, each showing different videos that have made their way to them after going viral online.

Damn.

I barely recognize myself as I watch scenario after humiliating scenario. What was I thinking getting so wasted and acting the way I did?

"My personal favorite is the one where you're on the roof pissing into the swimming pool," snickers Liam, one of the wide receivers.

"No, no," interrupts our fullback, Aiden. "The ones of you grinding against a stop light were a nice touch."

Each team member then chips in painfully, offering their opinion over which of my antics that night was their favorite. This is something I will never live down.

"Guys, come on," cuts in Brad, thankfully coming to my rescue. "Let's give the guy a break ... we all know the one where he stripped to the YMCA in the middle of that club was the winner."

So much for having my back.

The guys all begin howling with laughter, unable to hold it in any longer. It's ok for them, they aren't the ones who are about to have their careers decimated by YouTube. When they eventually finish riding my ass, I groan in embarrassment, but think to myself it could be worse. Worse has happened to other NFL players. Hopefully, I will get away lightly.

All hope goes out the window when I catch Brad's mortified expression.

"Goddamn," he murmurs, his Southern twang only truly comes out when he's stressed which means this can't be good.

57

"Hit me with it."

I wince as he takes a deep breath, ready to let me know exactly how low I sank that night.

"You might have gotten away with all this if there wasn't a video of you motorboating the Commissioner of the NFL's daughter."

The rest of the team breakdown in laughter as they show each other the video which is the icing on the cake.

I remember that morning, waking up feeling completely disorientated and concerned I couldn't recall a thing that happened. Brad convinced me everything would be fine, and I was simply suffering from post-alcohol memory loss. Nothing could have prepared me for my own real-life version of The Hangover. There's no way I'm going to be able to worm my way out of this one. Coach and the NFL are going to be furious and there are going to be some serious repercussions for that night.

"It'll be fine," Brad says quietly, as if he can read my mind.

Normally I'd believe him, but when the locker room door bangs open so loud the whole team jump out of their skin, I know there's no hope.

"Becket," Coach barks and my body flinches.

He spins on his heel back out of the locker room, anger flying off him in all directions. Slowly, I lift myself from the bench and sheepishly make my way to his office.

When I enter, I go to sit down in one of the chairs opposite him at his desk, but he holds up a hand. He's usually good at internalizing his anger, but not today. I've never seen him so mad as he visibly shakes, making me swallow nervously.

"Please explain why I have over ten YouTube videos of you blowing up my cellphone."

"I was wasted." My voice comes out barely a whisper. There's one person that puts the fear of God in the whole team despite our size and strength, and that's Coach.

"Well, that's obvious. Which part of your contract do you not understand? The part where it says you will behave yourself or the part where it says you can't act in a publicly indecent way? Because you've breached both clauses. In fact, no. You haven't just breached them … you've smashed them out of the ballpark."

"Baseball reference?" I smirk.

"Don't push me boy."

So much for making light of the situation.

"Sorry," I mutter.

He lets out a deep breath and I acknowledge how much older he seems. The stress of managing a team of guys like he does will do that to you.

"What happened?"

"Honestly?" He nods angrily, letting me know he expects nothing but the truth. "I can't remember anything. I got more drunk than planned."

"This is beyond drunk. Some of the things you do in these videos is downright reckless. I might've expected it from some of the other team members, but not you."

"I know. I don't know what I was thinking." I look down to the ground, feeling like a child being scorned by their parent.

"That much is obvious."

My shoulders sag with disappointment in myself. Today has added to the shit show that has become my life.

Coach must see the defeat written on my face as he says, "I'm pissed, I'm not gonna lie. I'm also disappointed in you and I expected better. But we will fix this together. Luckily, it's the only indiscretion you've had and hopefully the NFL will recognize that too."

"Ok." There's not much else I can say, which is why I don't say anything at all.

There's also the fear if I do, he will drag me back out to the field and make me run more drills as punishment.

"Promise me one thing ..."

"Yeah?"

"This is the worst of it over with."

"I promise ..."

Eight

The following weeks pass uneventfully and the media hype following my stint on YouTube quietens. Meanwhile I keep my head down and focus on one thing only, football. I'm a lucky son of a bitch and somehow don't wind up thrown out of the NFL. I've no doubt it's down to the efforts of Coach, so when he puts me through the ringer at each practice, I don't complain because it's nothing I don't deserve.

We're getting closer to the season opening and each day the pressure increases to the point of breaking us, yet somehow, as a team, we manage to keep going and push through. One day after practice, the guys and I venture out for lunch to celebrate surviving another brutal week of training. Having kept a lower profile than normal, it's the first time I've ventured out since the videos went viral.

It should be a celebration, but the party is over before it begins when the door to the restaurant flies open and I lock eyes with my PR agent Shauna, who's carrying a pile of media articles almost as big as she is. She storms over to the table where I'm sitting and throws down article after article on the table in front of me.

Smirking, I say, "Have they finally realized I'm a ball playing God?"

Some of the guys snort, trying to hold in their laughter as I poke the bear with a stick. Everyone knows not to mess with Shauna as she can make or break your career. The way she looks at me now, steam virtually coming out of her ears, I realize she doesn't need to do anything. It's already happening and out of our control.

"You wish," she spits. "Look down, Michael."

I feel like a child, not wanting to do as she says, scared of what I will find. It was a shitshow following the videos going viral and the media rode my ass hard. I thought I was getting a second chance at life when I managed to set foot on solid ground as I stepped off that godforsaken plane, but really it was just the beginning of the end for me.

My life continues to spiral out of control, one fuck up at a time.

I thought the videos alone were enough to decimate my career and that things couldn't get any worse. Finally, I look down. My eyes glance over the headlines and I choke on air as I absorb the words in front of me.

'Drug Fiend', 'Cheat', 'Heartbroken Wreck', just a few that my eyes settle on.

"What the fuck?" I carry on staring, aghast at what is in front of me.

"*What the fuck?* indeed." Shauna jams a stubby, manicured finger into my chest.

Looking up into her heavily made-up face, the phrase *pig in lipstick* comes to mind. I want to say as much and knock the bitch down a level for the way she's looking at me and treating me like a child in front of the rest of my team, but one last article catches my eye.

Shoving her hand out the way, I lean forward, and grab hold of the magazine, reading the headline that takes over most of the front page.

'Michael Becket Assault Case.'

I look around to see if the guys have seen it all. The way none of them look me directly in the face tells me what I need to know. The words ring over and over in my head. The games are over. Any funny element to all of this is gone.

Nobody knows about any of this, nobody. It was swept under the rug years ago thanks to having been a minor and a hefty amount of money involved in putting it to bed. However, it appears my secrets are coming to light thick and fast, and there's nothing I can do about it.

Most of the guys stand, and make to leave, some giving me a pat on the back or firm grip on the shoulder as a show of solidarity. Then the only people left are me, Shauna, and Brad. Shauna pulls out one of the now vacant chairs in front of me, plonking herself down then looking at me sternly.

"What the hell is happening with you Becket? Never in the years I've known you have I had to deal with any shit and now it's like a frickin' avalanche."

I frown at the headlines facing me. I should be mortified, angry, full of hate and wanting revenge, but I don't feel any of those things.

What I feel is confused.

"How do they know?" I ask myself quietly, at a loss.

Everyone knows the media is either lies or an embellishment of the truth, but these, are not.

Brad asks, "Is it true, man?"

I know which headline he's referring to, the one that has the potential to end my NFL career.

I nod in response, incapable of doing anything else. This is one secret that was never meant to resurface. The implications of the world knowing are huge, not for myself but the ones I've spent years trying to protect and hide, so they can live as normally as possible. It's what they deserved after everything they went through. My mind backtracks, focusing on one thing.

Nobody knew.

This was hidden in a sealed police document, there was no possible way somebody could have known.

Then it hits me.

"That bitch!" I roar, slamming my hand down on the table with such force it's surprising the wood doesn't crack. Shauna and Brad flinch but don't say anything as I begin ranting to myself. "I knew something was wrong as soon as I saw the headlines. Something didn't add up and now it makes sense why. They couldn't have uncovered all this shit and they didn't."

"What do you mean?" Brad looks at me like I've completely lost the plot.

"They were told." I stand, clenching my fists at my sides trying to contain my anger.

"By who?"

"Britney."

"Like *the* Britney?"

"Not quite, but she's the same level of crazy."

***

It's been two days since the media blew up in my face. Of all the headlines, the drug and assault related ones caused the biggest problems. They're the two things in football that can follow you around like a bad smell and have the worst influence on your career. The NFL hate it when things like this happen because it taints their reputation.

Sometimes things like this happen and there's legitimacy to the coverage, meaning the NFL come down hard on those involved. Not this time though. The past couple of days have been spent making sure it was clear the secrets being uncovered were from years ago, before my football career began. The last thing I need is an investigation and probing into my past, for more things to come to light.

They're called secrets for a reason.

I have Shauna and Coach to thank for everything. After she confronted me with the articles, Shauna scheduled an emergency meeting with Coach, where we came up with a plan to save my ass and put everything to bed. There's a reason I pay Shauna as much as I do. She squashed the rumors quickly, like they were an annoying fly. Without their quick thinking, I'd be drowning my sorrows in a bar, throwing my hard-earned money in the gutter, one drink at a time. No one needs to know the truth, only us.

"You're a lucky son of a bitch," Liam throws out.

We're in the locker room getting cleaned up after another of Coach's killer practices which have become a sick form of punishment. Unfortunately, the team is paying my dues in the form of extra drills. When you're part of a team, everyone suffers for one person's actions. I'm not the first to make a mistake and it isn't the first time our poor, achy bodies have been put through the ringer.

"Don't remind me," I grumble, trying to hide a wince as I bend over and attempt to dry myself. My body is broken and in need of a hot bath, a massage and a couple of days' undisturbed sleep. I make a second attempt to dry my legs, before giving up and collapsing on the bench in front of my locker. "This is brutal."

"Yeah, we know," scoffs Brad, hobbling from the shower area looking in a worse state than myself. "Only one person to thank for that."

He chuckles showing there's no hard feelings. Like the media storm, this too will pass.

"Do you know who did all this?" asks Aiden.

"I have an idea." My nostrils flare as I try not to lose control of my temper.

"Let me guess, some crazy bitch? Shit like this always comes down to the pussy."

Thankfully, there aren't hidden mics in here. The locker room is scoured daily by security for this very reason. If the public knew some of the crap that comes out of the guys' mouths, we wouldn't have a career. In the past I prided myself on my clean slate compared to the others. Not anymore.

"It's done with now," I say.

I want the conversation to end, not needing any reminders of the hellish few weeks I've had. It all began when I stepped on that plane to New York. There's a reason I hate the city, it's a jinx to my life.

"Good,' replies Aiden. "I don't think my ass can take a beating like that on the field for a while. You sure there's nothing else to come out? Do we need to prepare?"

I narrow my eyes, signaling he needs to shut his mouth. My control over my anger is teetering on the edge and there's only so much deep breathing I can do. He shakes his head and turns away, feebly getting himself changed, something I should do myself.

All I can focus on are his words. Is there anything else which could come out?

As far as I'm aware, psycho Britney did a thorough job digging up my skeletons. Unless something happened that I'm unaware of, there's no more dirty laundry to air. I've learnt my lesson and this chaos has confirmed why, over the years, I've always kept my head down and avoided any trouble.

All it takes is one wrong move for everything to come undone in this world.

I've been fooled once ... I won't be fooled again.

Nine

Living life in the NFL is harder than anyone knows. We live and breathe football. Our days are packed with drills, training, physiotherapy, and strength sessions. When we're not putting our bodies through some kind of torture, it's our minds taking over the punishment, learning an endless stream of plays, needing to know each move our bodies will make. Then there's the hours spent studying other players before each game, knowing their strengths and weaknesses better than we know our own.

Most days, every minute is accounted for, on the clock constantly, a never-ending slog. Today has been one of those days, but it's finally coming to an end.

Heading into my open plan kitchen, I place the bag of takeout I picked up on the way home on the table. The bland, carb free food isn't making my mouth water. What is though is the bottle of Scotch I have stored for emergencies.

I haven't so much as thought about alcohol since the night everything went wrong, but there's something about today. I need something to settle my mood, something only hard liquor will do. Grabbing a glass tumbler, I fill it with a generous amount, then go about emptying the trays of food onto a plate before heading, liquor and food in hand, to the couch.

The first drink goes down a treat. If it were a beer, I'd have necked it in one. We may have had a brutal day, but there are still early morning drills tomorrow. The punishment from Coach is never ending, so this one drink, albeit a large one, is all I'm allowed to nurse my wounds.

I've avoided thinking about Britney since the night I returned from New York, not wanting to let my thoughts wander back to her, afraid of where it will take me and what it will make me feel. She's undoubtedly the one who pulled this shit and left me in the gutter for the media to eat alive. I should hate her, but my mind still wanders back to that night in the restroom, remembering how she tasted, how she felt. Her soft creamy skin in my hands. The vanilla honey smell masked by the spicy perfume which invaded my senses.

At first, I thought she was as sassy as the attitude she put out, but in those moments when we thought we were about to die, she was a sweetheart through and through. Little did I know she had me fooled and how wrong I could be. Still, it doesn't change my body's uncontrollable reaction to thoughts of her. I can feel the stirrings of a hard on as I wonder what she would have felt like naked in my arms, driving into her and making her cry out in ecstasy.

I don't get long to indulge in my fantasies. As I'm contemplating calling it a night and heading to bed where my hand can finish the job, the doorbell rings, snapping me back to reality.

Who the hell would turn up on my doorstep at this time of night?

I sit, wondering whether it's a good idea to answer even with my high-tech security system in place. What would be the possibility of it being some crazed, diehard fan?

Telling myself I'm a pussy, and not the good kind that I'd love to bury myself deep inside, I just about convince myself to stand and open the door when sounds on the television stop me in my tracks. The doorbell long forgotten.

The news anchor, speaks out, her voice echoing around the room as she says, *'Breaking news just in.'* She rattles off some spiel about the content being sensitive to younger viewers. What I don't expect, is an image of me to flash up on the screen, on one of Florida's biggest news stations.

My heart rate increases tenfold causing me to break out in a cold sweat. I try my best to calm my mind and think about the past couple of weeks and everything I've done, rationally, before panic can settle in. There have been no benders, no blackouts. I've trained, eaten, slept. Unless I've taken up a habit of sleep walking and getting up to no good in the hours in which I'm unconscious, I haven't got a clue what I could have done to land me on prime-time news.

Nothing could prepare me for what comes next.

The room fills with the sounds of a woman moaning and hot, damp flesh slapping together. There's the odd moan and my eyes settle on what is very obviously me, as I shout out like a fool, *'Yeah baby just like that. You know how I like it. So good.'*

I sound like a frickin' porn star.

The sounds fill the room relentlessly. It's painful, but I can't take my eyes off the screen or make my ears unhear part of a night I've not been able to remember, no matter how hard I've tried. The only glimmer of hope is that the focus of the video is slightly off. Maybe Shauna, in all her PR glory, can spin this in my favor and make out that it's not me. What little hope there was, goes out the window, as the video adjusts, zooming in on my face as I come inside the beautiful brunette straddling me for the world to now see.

I let out a roar of frustration, as my body involuntarily lurches from the couch in anger. Swinging my arms, I sweep my plate of food and tumbler of Scotch off the table in front of me with such a force, that they shatter as they hit the wall. They're the least of my worries.

My cell begins lighting up and vibrating, the constant beep taunting me and making everything feel worse. It's the world wanting to know when I made a sex tape and why I was such an idiot to allow it to be leaked on national television. An image of Britney flashes through my mind, I'm not sure why, but somehow, I know she had something to do with all this.

Having been distracted by my life crumbling apart a little bit more, I forgot about the late-night visitor on my doorstep. The doorbell ringing incessantly once again, serves as a reminder and the way it continues relentlessly lets me know whoever it is, they are no longer willing to be patient.

I don't think about what I'm doing in my sorry and confused state, as I make my way through the lower level of my home to the front door. I forget that I'm not expecting any visitors and therefore don't have a clue who could be waiting, and the risks involved answering. It could be some crazy fan or worse a murderer. The way my luck is going, one of the two would be a better option, saving me from the train wreck that has become my life.

The door feels heavier than usual as I drag it open, my problems weighing down on me in such a way that they take away any physical strength I have left. And then I stand, gawping at the last person I expected to be standing in front of me.

"Lola?" I scoff at the costar in what is now our world-famous porn movie.

"Inside. Now!" She snaps.

Before I have a chance to ask what the urgency is, the screech of a media van, pulling around the corner in what is supposed to be my private community, brings me back to reality. I don't think about what I do next.

For someone who's lived their life relatively low-key and out of the limelight, despite being a major NFL player, the last couple of weeks have served as excellent practice for these sorts of scenarios. I stride quickly around the house, closing blinds and curtains wherever I can, blocking the world out. Closing the last ones, I feel somewhat in control.

I then head back to the kitchen where I left Lola, standing, and watching in horror as our sex tape plays on a loop on the television.

Rookie mistake.

There is no sign of the gentle girl I woke up next to. The one who looked hopeful when we parted ways, that our night of passion might have become something more. She's virtually unrecognizable, her stance cold and aggressive. It takes a moment for my brain to catch up with the burning sensation on my cheek, where she slaps me with all her might.

"What the fuck did you do?" she snarls.

I stand and rub at my jaw, attempting to relieve the sting while trying not to wince.

"I didn't do anything," I say. "I'm as shocked as you are."

She narrows her eyes. "Right ... after everything that's come out over the past few weeks, you shouldn't be surprised that I don't believe you."

I shrug and walk away, not caring to get into an argument. Whether she believes me or not is her choice. I have bigger things to worry about.

I reach up and retrieve another glass, filling it with whiskey. "Drink?"

She shakes her head angrily. "I didn't come here to be chummy. I came to find out what the hell is going on."

"I told you, I didn't do a thing."

"What a load of crap. There were two of us in that room and I know for certain that I didn't make a sex tape and leak it to the media."

I don't know why, maybe it's a defense mechanism kicking in when I say, "You should have. The performance you put on was stellar. You could make it big."

I even shock myself at the words that come out of my mouth and if I didn't already feel like shit, watching her demeanor crumble and tears stream down her face makes me feel worse than ever. I've officially hit an all-time low.

"Shit. I'm sorry." I want to reach out and comfort her, but nothing I do or say could fix this, it's all too raw.

"Why did you do this to me?" she sobs.

This isn't just about my own undoing, it's about hers as well. I'm not the only one who's life will be ruined because of this.

I hold my hands up, and for the first time since she walked through the door, I try to come across as an honest and genuine human being.

"Lola ... I promise, this wasn't me. None of this was. The past couple of weeks have been a mess and this is the icing on the cake. I promise that despite what you might think, I'm not that kind of guy and I didn't have any part to play in this."

After a while she sniffles, the surge of emotion seems to have passed, but the coldness in her eyes tells me I'm far from forgiven.

"So, who did?"

With excellent timing, the silent room is filled once more with the loud moans and groans of our night together.

"Fuck's sake," I mumble to myself as I scour the room for the remote control to turn the television off. We don't need to be reminded of our newfound fame. "I don't know, but I promise, when I find out there will be hell to pay. I'm sorry this happened to you."

She sniffles again. "You need to find out who did this and quick. Otherwise, it's your ass that's going through the grinder. You've messed with the wrong girl."

"I just told you I don't know who did it. Why am I now the one to blame?"

"Because if you can't find who did it, then you're next in line."

She spins on her heel, flicking her long brown hair over her shoulder, sashaying out of the room.

"Feel free to let the door hit you in the ass on the way out," I snap after her.

"I heard that," she calls over her shoulder. "That's another strike against you Michael Becket. Watch your back."

The door slams but sadly doesn't knock her down as she exits the house. I slump down on the couch, resigned after the shittest hour of my life. My cell continues lighting up and bleeping on the table, but I choose to ignore it, wondering what I'm going to do.

In a few short weeks I've wracked myself up quite a list. I've lost the person I thought was the love of my life to a pansy rock star. I've almost died in a plane crash. I've met a woman I thought I had a connection with, only to wake up the next day with another one entirely.

My life has panned out to the media like a sequel to The Hangover and when I thought it couldn't get any worse, I've become Florida's newest male porn star. When the NFL catches wind of this, I'm going to be out of a job, but I have a bigger problem on my hands, and her name is Lola.

The NFL has nothing on her.

They say hell hath no fury like a woman scorned. If that's the case, I'm screwed.

Acknowledgements

Never in my life did I ever think I would write one round of acknowledgements, let alone two, yet here we are and shock horror, this won't be the last.

Firstly, thank you to Peter for all the late nights of moral support, never once complaining that I wasn't paying you any attention (well maybe there was a little bit of complaining), and being on Daddy Duty when I needed to, "quickly get a few words done", only to still be writing hours later.

Thank you to my girls, who once again adapted to the crazy scenario that was Mummy writing *another* book during a pandemic and enduring all the extra Hey Duggee time.

Thank you to my Mum, for taking the girls off my hands when you got a chance and giving me the extra time, needed to make this dream a reality.

Thank you to Babs, for once again being the first set of eyes on another piece of my work and giving me your honest feedback and support.

Thank you, Sarah, for ploughing through the proofing even though I'm sure there were a million other things you would have rather been doing. I now owe you at least two bottles of wine.

Finally, thank you to you, the reader and everyone who bought the first book, Always You. Without your encouragement and wonderful feedback, I don't think I would have been as inspired to write another part of Abby and Jake's journey.

I hope you're all as excited as I am to see where life takes them next.

Fool Me Twice

I have one regret in life: fooling Michael Becket, the most promising quarterback in the NFL.

He was supposed to be a simple job, a chance to put the past behind me. It turned into a media scandal which left him famous for all the wrong reasons.

They say keep your enemies close. Becket and I got too close, and something lurking in the shadows proved why we could never be together.

There were secrets.

Too many.

Whose were the darkest, only time will tell.

Read on for a sneak peak of the next book in the
series!

LIZZIE MORTON

Prologue

Britney 18 years old

I quickly open my bag to pull out my lunch. Something feels off as I stare down inside at the contents. I sit and blink, trying to put my finger on what it is, and then it hits me. I've forgotten my gym kit, the same gym kit I need for my next class. *Damn it.* This is the third time I've forgotten it this semester. I'm screwing up left, right, and center. Nobody would blame me, but still ... I need to do some damage control. I'm burning through my free passes, and I can't afford to run out.

I give the measly lunch package in my bag a longing look, not that it deserves it. It consists of a sandwich made with five-day-old bread I had to pick the mold off and half a granola bar I salvaged from the floor, next to where my mom was passed out on the couch. It's the first thing I'll have eaten all day and my stomach groans painfully.

I sigh and close my bag. Food will have to wait.

The woman sitting at the desk in the school office gives me a disdainful look when I explain why I need to leave. *Whatever.* She's the least of my worries and if I stand a chance of getting home and back before next period, I can't mess around.

Outside, I pull out my cell and try one last time to get in touch with Ross. It goes straight to voicemail. Helpful ... *not.*

Time is ticking away.

I'd sprint, but my shitty sneakers have no cushioning, and the last time I had to run in them I was hobbling for days. I opt for power walking as fast as I can. I cannot get detention. I have a shift at the diner tonight and the paycheck is the only thing keeping a roof over our heads, and the meals that are few and far between, on the table.

This would all have been easier if Ross had just answered his cellphone. I know he had a couple of free periods and could have run home to grab my stuff, that's if I'd been able to get in touch with him. When I reach our apartment, I unlock the door and rush to my room, grabbing my gym kit off the bed that I stupidly forgot to pack.

I hear a noise. A groan.

I stop in my tracks and listen for a few seconds. Nothing. I must have been hearing things. I'm about to turn and leave, when I hear it again. This time a moan accompanies the groan. It's louder and I know it's not my imagination. The smart thing would be to call out, warn whoever is in the apartment that I'm here. With Mom, you never know who she could have let through the door. But I'm too focused on finding out what is going on.

I should walk away and ignore it, but I don't.

Tiptoeing into the living area, my eyes flicker to the couch where Mom was out cold when I left this morning. She's not there. I walk quietly to her room, a task that should be easy, but proves difficult—each time I lift a foot my shoe sticks to the carpet and I

82

struggle not to fall. The door is ajar, and the noises get louder the closer I get.

When I push the door open, I stop.

If my world hadn't fallen apart years ago, this would do it.

Dumbfounded, I watch as Ross, my childhood sweetheart and the only person I thought was left in my life who I could trust, groans while my mom sits on top of him, riding him like she's auditioning for a porn movie.

I clap a hand over my mouth, trying to stifle the gasp that comes out. It's wasted effort on my part, because on the floor are two syringes and a tourniquet. I could make all the noise in the world—they're both too high to care.

I want to look away, but I'm transfixed. It wasn't enough that she fucked up her life, she had to go and destroy the only good thing I had going in mine. Nausea hits when I back away.

I'm done.

I run to my room and shove what little belongings I have left—the ones I haven't already had to sell—into a bag. Without so much as a backward glance, I storm out of the apartment, leaving my pathetic excuse of a life behind.

One

Britney 6 years later

"Britney! Into my office ... now!" Fiona screeches across the room.

Staring at the screen of my laptop, I grimace. *Again?*

I purposefully fly under her radar. All I want is to get on with my job in peace. Despite my best efforts, I keep getting dragged into 'projects' that are anything but peaceful. I've learned the hard way that gossip doesn't appear out of nowhere, and I work for the most raucous gossip magazine in the country. I've worked here for a little over a year and it's safe to say I've hated every minute.

"Be right there," I chime over my shoulder, being careful not to let her see my face.

"Leigh, you too!" she screeches again, as if we're not all squashed together in a room like sardines.

Leigh, at the desk two over from me, sighs. Everyone knows when you get called into Fiona's office, it's bad news ... excuse the pun.

I *hate* this. I worked my ass off to get into college, managed to achieve a scholarship with no support behind me, and this is where I've found myself after years of hard work. If I could be anywhere but here, I would. Unfortunately, I have no choice. Firstly, there's a nice backlog of college fees hanging over me, but they're the least of my worries. When Mom disappeared off the grid not long after I walked out, she still owed a lot of people money. Like *a lot* of money, to the kind of people who don't let debts slide. They couldn't find her, but they found me, thanks to my name being added to our final rental contract when I turned eighteen.

So, now, I work for the devil.

I spend my days chasing celebrities, watching their every move, trying to get the latest scoop. We sell their mistakes and obliterate any hope they might have for a bit of normality. Each time I write an article, I can't shake the feeling that one day this is all going to come back and bite me in the ass. Karma is coming, I just know it.

Saving the piece I've been working on about some lame middle-aged guy sleeping with the nanny, I reluctantly head to Fiona's office to find out what she wants. When I arrive, Leigh is already settled in the only chair available. I'm left standing awkwardly at her side waiting for Fiona to reveal what delightful project she has in store for us next. Twiddling my hands in front of me, my eyes flicker to the wall behind where Fiona is sitting. It's filled with framed covers of some of the magazine's best-selling issues. The issues in which we've done our worst.

"I have a new project for you," Fiona says, as if we're going to be creating a masterpiece, building something great, changing the world. Not destroying someone's life.

Biting on my cheek, it takes everything in me to keep my expression pleasant.

"There's a rumor that the NFL player Becket is having problems with his girlfriend," Fiona continues.

"I hate to break it to you ..." says Leigh, tossing her fiery red hair over her shoulder, "that's not exactly gossip. It's also not surprising considering what a prick he is. And he's boring. He puts the straight in strait-laced."

I remain standing quietly as Fiona narrows her eyes at Leigh. "I'm perfectly aware of that. Which is why you are both here. As I was saying ... there's a rumor circling that he's having issues with his girlfriend and apparently, he is on his way to the city. Someone saw him checking in for a flight to New York from Florida and posted the photo on Instagram. I want you to follow him when he gets here—get whatever scoop you can. This could be big."

Brazenly, Leigh responds, "If we do *whatever it takes*, what do we get in return? I'm assuming this might be a little out of our pay grade?"

Fiona pauses before replying and I wonder if for once, Leigh has pushed her luck too far. "A bonus and a step up the ladder. How does that sound?"

Leigh's mouth drops open. "All for Becket the Bore?"

My eyes dart back and forth between them, I daren't say a word, afraid that if I do, she might change her mind. The worst part about the crap she has us do: the pay isn't worth it. It's still more than I'd get in most other jobs at this level. Even in a city as big as New York, jobs like this are hard to come by. The offer she's put on the table could finally make all this worthwhile, it could be a chance to move away from doing this crap *and* pay off a large chunk of my debts.

Fiona leans back in her seat, looking bored. "It's been a long time since there's been an NFL scandal. The best ones are unexpected. I want us to be the first ones reporting when it comes out and there's only one way to make sure we are ..."

"How can we?" I ask. "It's never a given."

Leigh looks up at me and rolls her eyes. I feel like even more of an idiot, but unlike to her, all this stuff doesn't come naturally to me.

"We make sure we're there when it happens—that we know about it before everyone else," Leigh says.

I still don't quite get what it is they're both suggesting. "You sound so certain. What if there's no dirt to dig up and what if there's no scandal?" I ask.

Leigh and Fiona look at each other with amused expressions.

Fiona replies, "If there's no scandal to be found ... you make one."

***

"I can't believe we're stuck doing her dirty work again," I say bitterly, scrolling through page after page on the internet, familiarizing myself with the life of *The Great Michael Becket*.

Leigh's right, he's as boring as they come. His girlfriend, his stats—perfect. He's a shining star in the NFL as far as his performance is concerned. But it's like someone went through Google and deleted anything that would give him any character or depth. He has no past. The best I can find are articles about him saying the wrong thing or being a hot head on the field.

Basically, when he's not running the perfect play ... he's an asshole.

It's the images that really capture my attention. Page after page, thousands of them. The one thing they all have in common: his eyes. A glimmer of emerald reaching out to me in every single one. But there's something there. Even in the most unclear ones, I can see something is amiss. There's a darkness battling the light in his eyes, and I want to know why.

Leigh spins around in her desk chair. It's late and everyone, including Fiona, has gone home for the day. Now, it's just us left, trying to figure out how we're going to magic up some scoop. I've come up with nothing, I never do, because unlike the redhead next to me, I don't thrive off being deceitful.

"Suck it up," she says. "There's a promotion on the cards and I won't let you mess this up for me." Her expression is cold. She's ruthless and would do anything to move up the career ladder, if you can even call what we're doing a career. An alert flashes on her screen and she turns back quickly to see what it is. She sits quietly reading, then shouts out loud, "Yes!"

"Care to share?" I ask.

"There's a forum we use sometimes when we need a scoop on people." She begins scribbling on a scrap of paper.

"And?"

"And somebody has just responded, saying they have details on Becket. Where he's going to be et cetera."

I stare at her in disbelief as she grabs her bag and stands up.

Before leaving, she looks at me and asks, "What?"

"Never mind the fact you're going to trust a random stranger, but you're going to meet with them too?"

She rolls her eyes, something she does a lot of whenever we work together. "The forum is legit. I use it all the time. This is how we play the game, but you wouldn't know because you never get your hands dirty."

"Huh, I'd say the opposite. So, what's the plan?"

"You wait here. I'll be twenty minutes, max. They're meeting me outside."

She doesn't wait for me to respond or acknowledge that I'm happy to do so, simply bustles out of the office. I now have another person who thinks they can walk all over me. Great.

True to her word she walks back twenty minutes later with a smug look on her face.

"So?"

"So, our source is freakin' amazing! They know everything about him. We don't need to do anything but turn up where he says."

"You're not worried that this person knows Becket's every move?"

She throws her head back and laughs. "No. It makes our jobs easier. Stop overthinking it and just play the game, Britney. We follow him, catch him doing something newsworthy, and it's a job done. Although some interference might be necessary."

My stomach twists. "What do you mean interference?"

She slides open her desk drawer, grabs something, then holds a packet of little white pills in the air.

"What the fuck, Leigh?" I hiss, then smack her hand down in case anyone is lingering in the office who could see and report us. "Are you trying to get us fired?"

"Chill out," she huffs. "It's nothing they haven't seen before. How do you think we get so many good stories?" I watch as she slides the packet back into her drawer.

I shake my head. "What are you talking about? And why are you not putting them in your bag?"

"How do you think we always get the best gossip? Don't tell me you think it's all a coincidence? It's all set up. People here do what needs to be done. And I'm not putting the pills in my bag, because I can't exactly walk on a plane with drugs ..."

"Then where are you going to get them from when we touch down in Jacksonville?"

"Our source." She rolls her eyes again as if she can't believe the questions I'm asking her.

It comes out as almost a squeak when I say, "You're going to take drugs off a stranger?"

"Come on, Britney. Whoever you get drugs from is a stranger. Fact."

"So, we're just going to drug Becket? That's the plan?" I scoff.

"No. Not if we don't have to. Just go with the flow and let's see what happens. If we come up with nothing then we do as Fiona said: we make our own story. And something like this is what's going to help us along."

She waves the packet in front of my face again, taunting me, and I wonder exactly how deep I'm about to sink.

**

"Are you sure your source got it right?" I ask Leigh.

We're standing in the departure area of JFK airport, in the same spot we've been for the past hour, waiting for Becket to show up and check-in for a flight back to Florida. We followed him all day yesterday after Leigh's source informed us he was at Coney Island. Things between him and his girlfriend turned sour, and he stormed off. Thanks to it being packed with people celebrating the Fourth of July we were unable to follow him any further.

We thought we had royally screwed up, until Leigh received a message saying he had checked into a hotel in Manhattan for the night. The same source got in touch earlier today, informing us Becket had booked a flight out of New York. So, here we are. I keep trying to stamp down the feelings of unease that there's someone out there following his every move, even more so than we are. It's creepy as fuck but there's nothing I can do. I need this promotion, this money.

Leigh crosses her arms over her chest and frowns, looking around the crowds trying to spot him. "Stop bitching at me. I'm certain. And before you ask again, my source is reliable."

I grind my teeth, trying not to bite back. If we start arguing, we're going to draw attention to ourselves and we can't screw up again. Images of Leigh pulling out a sachet of white pills flash through my mind. "Did you bring that stuff with you?" My eyes dart around nervously.

She shakes her head. "Seriously, you need to calm down. You look shifty and if you keep it up, we're going to have security on our case."

"Do you blame me for asking?" I whisper. "Two days ago, you were waving drugs in my face. I don't know what to expect with you anymore."

"Yes, but I'm not an idiot. Give me some credit. You know what the plan is. Tease him on the flight, make him want you, then go for a drink together. I'll pick up the supply from the source when we land in Florida, then sneak it to you the first chance we get. You slip it in his drink and the rest is easy."

"The source is now going to be in Florida too. Who the hell is this guy?"

"Honestly, Britney, if you're not up to this then leave it to me, but you're definitely more his type. You scream ball bunny."

I want to slap her. Instead, I narrow my eyes and say, "Its fine, I can do it."

"You're sure? Forget the promotion—if you fuck this up, both our jobs will be on the line."

I nod. "I can do it."

A tall figure in the distance catches my attention. "Is that him?" I ask.

Leigh turns and her face lights up when she sees him. "I told you he'd be here."

With his cap pulled down low, his only recognizable feature is the strands of sandy colored hair peeking free. We don't need to look directly at him. The women passing by as they appreciate his broad frame, and the men trying to not so subtly take photos of one of the best players in the league, tell us what we need to know: it's him.

He turns in our direction and I suck in a sharp breath. Of course, Leigh doesn't miss my reaction to him, she never misses a thing.

"Not hating the job now, are you? There are worse things you could have to do than throw yourself at an NFL player. Just remember, this is work. It's a two-hour flight. Don't go falling for the guy."

"I get it, ok." I shrug her off and stand watching his retreating form as he moves through airport security.

Before we part and make our way to the plane separately, I repeat to myself what the plan involves. She's right, it's easy. Unfortunately, what isn't so easy is getting my heart rate under control as the image of him glancing up from under his ball cap firmly imprints itself in my mind.

OTHER WORK BY LIZZIE MORTON

Always Series:

Always You
Always Us
Always

Fool Me Series:

Fool Me Once
Fool Me Twice
Fool Me Thrice

Summer Nights Series:

Just One Kiss
Just One Night – Coming Soon
Just Once More – Coming Soon

Always You

Steer clear of her ex, Jake.

That's Abby West's goal when she returns to Brooklyn, following her heartbreak fueled, six-year hiatus.

The plan should be foolproof because her life's finally on track.

Photography career. Check.
Hot-shot NFL boyfriend. Check.

Unfortunately, the reason she left, all six foot plus, dark, handsome and deliciously tattooed inch of him, threatens to derail all the progress she's made. And when Abby is tasked with photographing Jake's rock band, who are on the path to success, avoiding him becomes impossible.

But one big secret and a huge betrayal still loom over Abby and Jake.

What follows is a summer of friendships rekindled, memories made, old feelings unearthed and the ultimate dilemma.

Do you ever really move on from the one that got away?

Always Us

Alone in Cape Town, Abby West is struggling to forget her return home to Brooklyn and questioning if she's made the right choice.

A whirlwind summer uproots her new life, and Abby and her friends find themselves unexpectedly on S.C.A.R.A.B.'s European music tour, surrounded by Rock Gods.

With Jake still refusing to give Abby the truth, and a chance meeting with a stranger thrown into the mix, it's a recipe for disaster.

But just when they think they might finally be able to move forward, the tables turn.

For Abby the decision is no longer between her head or her heart.

It's whether love, really is enough.

Always

Abby West's life is about to change, and she can't decide if it's for better or worse.

But Jake's career is about to take off, meaning the path she needs to take, might be one she has to walk alone.

Right before she hits rock bottom, the person Abby least expects gives her exactly what's needed, a break from reality.

Taking the chance, she leaves everything and everyone behind. But there's only so long she can hide from the truth, and when it comes out, it's explosive.

In the epic conclusion to Abby and Jake's story, their relationship is put to the ultimate test, and with both of their futures on the line, they have a final decision to make.

Were they ever meant to be together?

Printed in Great Britain
by Amazon